RhinO CORN

Elanor Best • Stephanie Thannhauser

make believe ideas

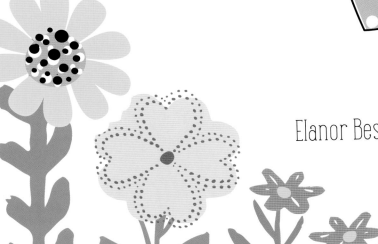

Riley believes with all of her HEART that you CANNOT tell her and her BEST FRIENDS apart.

She has a COOL TAIL, FOUR LEGS, and a HORN.

In **RILEY'S** view, she's a

UNICORN!

Her meals are all made up of
PINK LOLLIPOPS.

FIZZ-SHERBET TEA,
and SWEET CANDY DROPS.

When racing down RAINBOWS
she knows she will win...

WHEEEE!

...she PLUMMETS straight down with a big CHEESY grin.

One day, as **RILEY** was SKIPPING along,
she BUMPED into someone who looked
tough and **strong**.

Her eyes opened wide and
she let out a SCREAM:

"You're the
MOST GIANT
UNICORN
I've ever seen!"

Big Rocky laughed as he boomed, "That's not true!

I'm not a UNICORN... neither are you!

We're **RHINOS**, with four legs for **stomping** around.

Our tails **swat** at flies

and our horns
dig the ground."

RILEY thought NONE of those things sounded FUN
and decided to show **Rocky** how things were done.

"Our UNICORN horns
are the COOLEST of things.

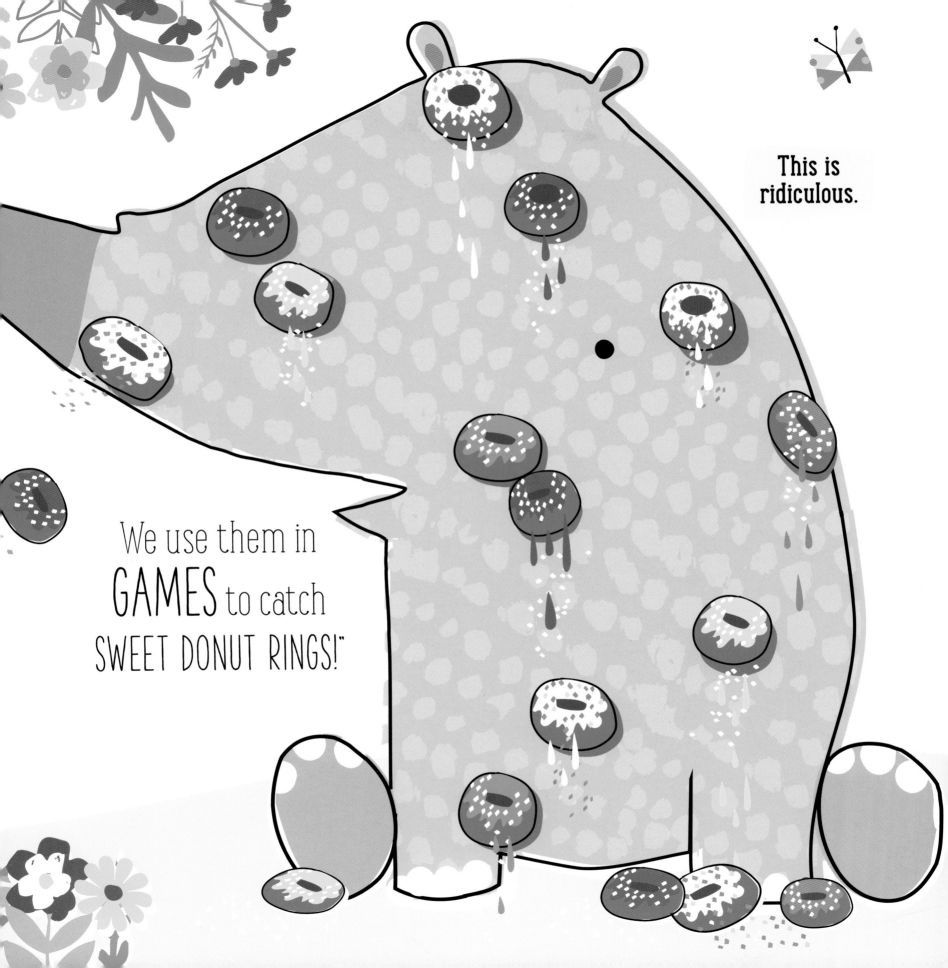

This is
ridiculous.

We use them in
GAMES to catch
SWEET DONUT RINGS!"

"Our UNICORN tails
are not what they seem.
With a MAGICAL FLICK,
they make RAINBOWS that GLEAM!"

Amazing.

"Our UNICORN legs are for dancing BALLET.
First, POINT your toes, then try a PLIÉ.

So with ALL that in mind,
I think you'll AGREE,

that we are as

'UNICORN'

as UNICORNS can be!"

Rocky HEMMED and he HAWED
and he SCRATCHED at his head.

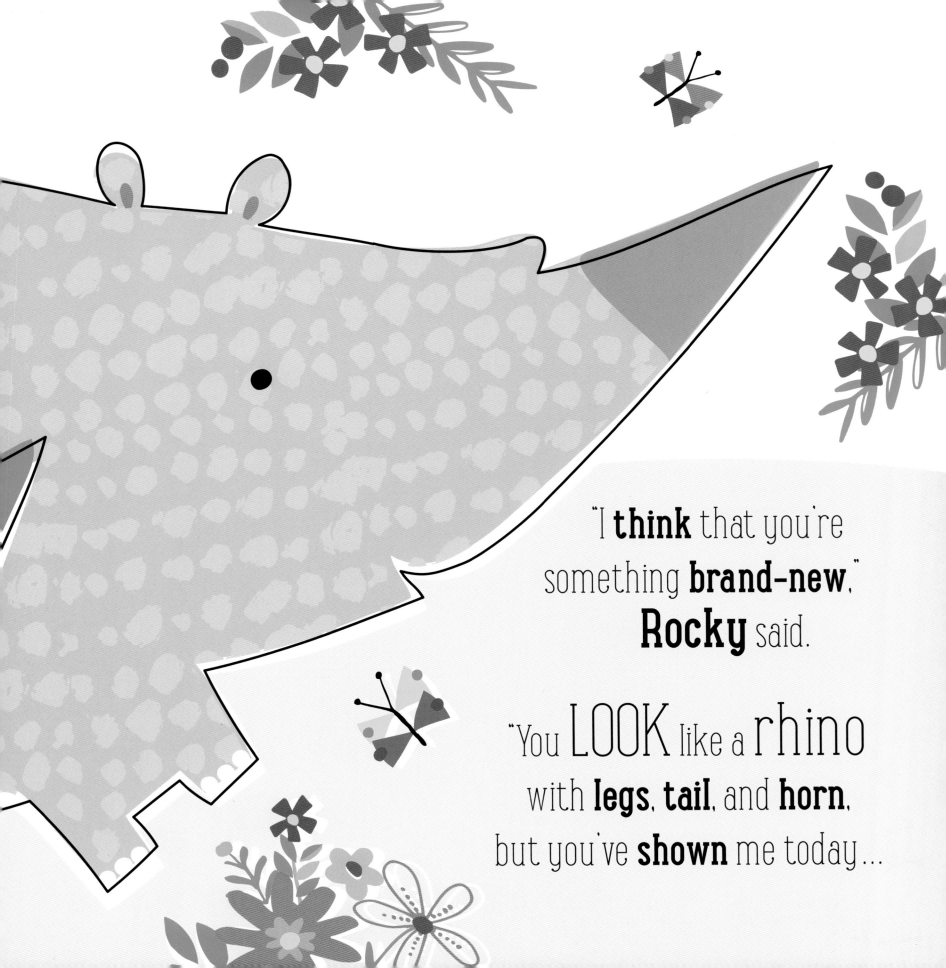

"I **think** that you're
something **brand-new**,"
Rocky said.

"You LOOK like a rhino
with **legs**, **tail**, and **horn**,
but you've **shown** me today...

CORN!

Half-rhino,
half-unicorn,
that's what you are.

You are **true** to yourself,
which is better by **far!**"

Rocky said,
"I've had so much **fun**,
playing with you.
I think that I **might** be
a Rhino CORN too."

Riley and Rocky then lived happily,

being as RHINOCORN as RHINOCORNS can be!